Delphie and the Magic Ballet Shoes
AND
Rosa and the Secret Princess

Welcome to the world of Enchantia!

I have always loved to dance. The captivating music and wonderful stories of ballet are so inspiring. So come with me and let's follow Delphie and Rosa on their magical adventures in Enchantia, where the stories of dance will take you on a very special journey.

p.s. Turn to the end of each story to learn a special dance step from me...

Special thanks to
Linda Chapman, Katie May
and Nellie Ryan

Delphie and the Magic Ballet Shoes first published by
HarperCollins *Children's Books* in 2008
Rosa and the Secret Princess first published by
HarperCollins *Children's Books* in 2009
This two-in-one edition first published in 2011
HarperCollins *Children's Books* is a division of HarperCollins*Publishers* Ltd,
77-85 Fulham Palace Road, Hammersmith, London W6 8JB

The HarperCollins website address is
www.harpercollins.co.uk

3

ISBN 978-0-00-741440-6

Printed and bound in England by
Clays Ltd, St Ives plc

Magic Ballerina

Delphie and the Magic Ballet Shoes

Darcey Bussell

HarperCollins *Children's Books*

*To Phoebe and Zoe, as they are the inspiration
behind Magic Ballerina.*

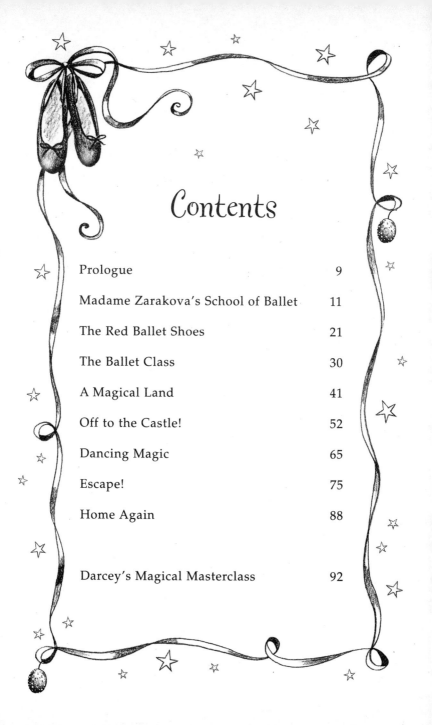

Contents

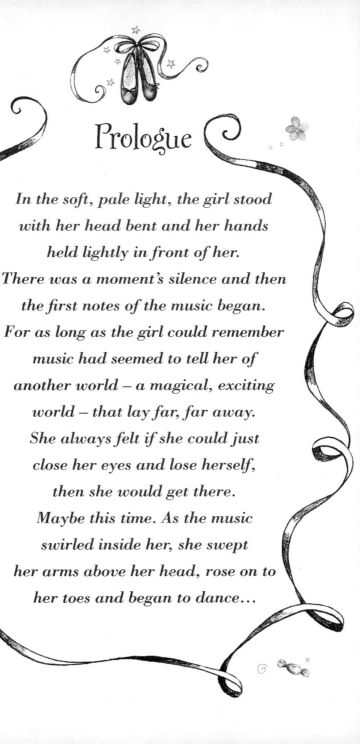

Prologue

*In the soft, pale light, the girl stood
with her head bent and her hands
held lightly in front of her.
There was a moment's silence and then
the first notes of the music began.
For as long as the girl could remember
music had seemed to tell her of
another world – a magical, exciting
world – that lay far, far away.
She always felt if she could just
close her eyes and lose herself,
then she would get there.
Maybe this time. As the music
swirled inside her, she swept
her arms above her head, rose on to
her toes and began to dance…*

Madame Zarakova's School of Ballet

Delphie hurried home, her breath freezing in the snowy night air. The houses on either side of the road had their curtains drawn – all apart from one – a big double-fronted house with iron railings and a gate. Two stone steps led up to the door and light streamed out of the windows. As the snowflakes landed softly on Delphie's shoulders, she looked longingly at the brass plate, just as she had for the last four weeks since it had been open: *Madame Zarakova's School of Ballet.*

A car drew up outside and two girls jumped out. They were about nine – the same age as Delphie – and had their hair tied back in neat buns.

"Come on, we're going to be late!" one of them called as they ran through the gate and opened the front door. "Madame Za-Za will go mad!"

For a moment, Delphie caught sight of a long wide hallway with white walls and wooden floors before the heavy door banged shut behind them.

Delphie felt a wave of longing so strong it hurt. She wanted to be inside the ballet school about to have a dance lesson. She was ballet-mad but her parents had always put her off having lessons.

"Maybe when you're a bit older," her mum had said, kissing Delphie's long dark hair. "The nearest dance school is on the other side of town. It's too far to take you every week."

But Delphie hadn't been put off. She had borrowed books from the library and practised ballet exercises almost every day. And she danced all the time – in the house, in the garden, she wasn't even embarrassed to dance on the street! She loved the feeling of spinning, moving, jumping. It was hard to explain but, although she had never had any lessons,

inside she just felt like she knew what it was like to be a real ballerina.

And now Madame Zarakova's ballet school had opened on the very street she lived. But even that hadn't helped her. Delphie did understand. After all, money was quite tight in their house.

"I'm sorry, sweetheart," Mrs Durand, Delphie's mum, had sighed. "We just can't afford to send you there."

Standing by the railings now, Delphie could now hear the faint sounds of a piano tinkling and, through the branches, she could see light from the big windows falling into the front garden. Shivering she pulled her coat closer around her as she looked over the railings.

The music and lights seemed to be calling her nearer. Slipping through the gate, she crept over to the house, peering in through the window. The room inside was large with mirrors on each of the four walls. Eight girls, all about the same age, were holding lightly to the *barre*, a wooden pole that was fixed around the wall of the room. They were all dressed in pink leotards with a ribbon round their waists, pale socks and satin ballet shoes with ribbons crossed neatly round their ankles.

They were gracefully bending and straightening their knees out over their toes.

"*Pliés*," Delphie sighed longingly, recognising them from one of her books. Oh, if only she could be in there with them.

Madame Za-Za was walking around the room, talking to the girls and correcting a leg position here, an arm position there. She held her own body erect and her grey-streaked brown hair was pulled back in a bun. As Delphie watched, the girls began a different exercise, pointing their toes and sliding their legs to the back, front and side. *Battements tendu*, thought Delphie. All the girls looked good but there was one dark-haired girl who looked very graceful and seemed to find everything very easy.

Next the girls began sliding the foot that was furthest from the *barre* and lifting it off the floor, stretching out as far as they could and holding their free arm out to the side.

Delphie couldn't resist. She began to join in.

Holding on to the windowsill, she performed the movement in time with the girls inside.

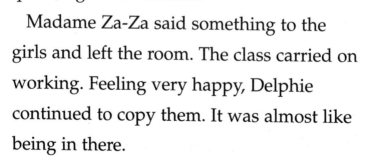

Sweeping her arm and leg to the side, she held them in perfect position, her toe pointed and heel raised from the ground. They moved quickly into practising quick, light movements.

Madame Za-Za said something to the girls and left the room. The class carried on working. Feeling very happy, Delphie continued to copy them. It was almost like being in there.

Then, suddenly, the front door swung open and a voice called out. "You, girl! What are you doing?"

Delphie jumped in shock and swung round. She had been concentrating so hard on the dancing that she hadn't heard it opening. It was Madame Za-Za standing on the top step, staring at her!

Delphie froze to the spot. "I… I'm really sorry! I just wanted to have a look."

"Come here, child!" Madame Za-Za called.

And with just a moment's hesitation, Delphie hurried up the steps.

The Red Ballet Shoes

"Come inside, child" Madame Za-Za said. "What is your name?"

"Delphie Durand." Delphie felt tears prickling her eyes. She was sure she was about to be told off. She blinked quickly; she hated crying in front of people.

"I saw you through the window,"

Madame Za-Za said to her. "Where do you learn ballet?"

Delphie was very surprised by the question. "I… I don't go to classes," she answered. "I just read about it in books and practise at home."

"I see." Madame Za-Za looked at her for a moment. "Well, why don't you come in?"

"Come in?" Delphie echoed.

Madame Za-Za nodded. "It's cold out
here and I think you would like to see
around. Am I right?"

"Yes!" Delphie gasped. "I'd love to see inside."

"Come, then."

Walking in a daze, Delphie followed
Madame Za-Za inside the school. They
went down the warm, brightly lit corridor.
"Here we have the dance studios," Madame
Za-Za explained, pointing to two rooms,
one on either side.

"Wow!" Delphie breathed.

Madame Za-Za looked thoughtfully at
her. "Do you have any ballet shoes, child?"

"No," Delphie replied. She always just
danced in bare feet.

Madame Za-Za gave a small nod and

then set off down a dark corridor, opening
a door at the end that led into a small
storeroom. The walls were covered with
shelves piled high with boxes, dusty books,
ballet costumes and what looked like a
chest full of new ballet leotards and socks.

Madame Za-Za went into the room and
took an old, battered box down from a high
shelf.

As Delphie watched, Madame Za-Za
opened the lid to reveal a pair of old red
leather ballet shoes with red ribbons, nestling
among yellowing tissue paper. The leather
was slightly crinkly, the insides of the shoes
a deep cream. They were worn and slightly
shabby but as Delphie looked at them, she
felt a sudden urge to reach into the box.

Her feet tingled as if they wanted to try them on.

Unable to stop herself she touched the soft red leather and then realising what she was doing, she pulled her hand back.

She looked up to see Madame Za-Za studying her face, her expression unreadable.

"Do you like them?" Madame Za-Za asked.
"Oh yes," Delphie breathed. The ballet
shoes might be old but
they were beautiful.
"Would you like
to borrow them,
child?" Madame
Za-Za asked gently.

"Borrow them!" Delphie stared in
surprise. "But why would you lend them to
me? I don't even come here to classes."

"If you like you can come back tomorrow
and join in with the class you were watching,"
Madame Za-Za said.

Delphie could hardly believe her ears.
"But… but… well, I'd love to but Mum and
Dad can't afford for me to have lessons." She

blushed as she admitted the truth.

Madame Za-Za waved her hand dismissively. "Money does not matter. Just come tomorrow as I ask." Her eyes met Delphie's. "I will teach you for free."

Delphie's mind spun.

"Go home now and tell your parents what I have said. They may ring me if they have any questions." Madame Za-Za gave her the box with the ballet shoes and then turned and took a brand-new pink leotard and socks out of the chest near the door. "Bring these clothes and the shoes to wear tomorrow."

Delphie looked down at the box in her arms. "What if the shoes don't fit me?"

Madame Za-Za gave a mysterious smile. "Oh, I don't think there will be a problem with that. I think you will find them the perfect size. They have been waiting for the right person to come along and something tells me you might be that person."

Her eyes stared deep into Delphie's. "They are very special shoes, Delphie. I

hope one day you find out just how special they are." Suddenly her tone became brisker. "Now, I must return to class. I will see you tomorrow, ready and changed for half past four sharp."

"Thank you!" Delphie gasped.

Almost before she knew it, she was following Madame Za-Za back down the corridor and then she was back outside in the snow again. But Delphie didn't feel cold. Excitement raced through her as she hugged the shoes to her chest. She rushed home to tell her Mum. She was going to start ballet classes tomorrow. She couldn't wait!

The Ballet Class

Delphie could hardly concentrate in school at all the next day. All she could think about was her first ballet lesson. She was at Madame Za-Za's school by four o'clock and had changed twenty minutes before the class was due to start.

As Delphie tied her long hair back into a bun, she looked at herself in the mirror and couldn't stop grinning. She looked just like

the girls she had been
watching the day before.
Well, apart from the fact
that her shoes were red
instead of pale pink but
Delphie didn't care about that.
They were beautifully soft and they fitted
her perfectly, just as Madame Za-Za had
said they would.

Other girls started to arrive. The two who
Delphie had seen running into the ballet
school the day before were the first to get
there. "Who are you?" one of them asked
curiously.

"I'm Delphie," Delphie replied.

"Are you just starting lessons here?" the
other girl asked.

Delphie nodded.

"Well, I'm Poppy," the first girl said.

"And this is Lola."

"Hiya Delphie," Lola smiled.

Other girls started to pile in. They were just as friendly and at half past four they all went into the dance studio where Madame Za-Za was waiting for them.

They began with *pliés* at the *barre*. Delphie concentrated hard, trying to remember everything she had read in her books.

As she followed Madame Za-Za's instructions, she felt herself relax and soon it was just as if she was practising in her bedroom at home but a hundred times better because she was in a real ballet class.

Madame Za-Za kept telling them all to keep their heads up and to smile but Delphie didn't find that difficult at all.

The girls moved from the *barre* to working

in the centre of the room. They went through the same exercises again and then practised arm movements, different poses and turns called pirouettes.

As they neared the end of the class, Madame Za-Za explained to Delphie that the class had been learning a dance from a ballet called *The Nutcracker*.

Delphie had read about *The Nutcracker* – a girl called Clara was given a nutcracker who looked like a soldier as a Christmas present by her uncle. Clara loved her new toy so much that she crept downstairs when everyone was in bed and danced with him before falling asleep.

"I think you had better just watch this bit of the class, Delphie," Madame Za-Za said to her. "The others have been learning the dance for a while now."

Delphie sat, feeling nervous, as the other eight girls took it in turns to hold a wooden doll which looked like a toy soldier and dance Clara's dance. The dark-haired girl, who Delphie had found out was called

Sukie, was the last to go. She moved very gracefully and didn't wobble on any of the positions she held. Her turns were easy and smooth

35

and her arms and head always seemed to
be held perfectly in position. But even so
there was something that wasn't quite
right. *What is it?* Delphie wondered.

Madame Za-Za was watching from near
the piano. As Sukie finished and smiled,
Madame Za-Za walked forward, shaking

her head. "No, Sukie, Your hands, your arms, your placing were all good, but you are supposed to love the doll you are holding. I did not believe that when I watched you."

Delphie realised she knew exactly what Madame Za-Za meant. Although Sukie's dancing had looked wonderful, she hadn't made Delphie feel like she was really watching Clara.

Madame Za-Za turned to all the girls. "Ballet is about much more than just dancing – the real magic comes from telling a story and making the audience believe in that story." Her eyes looked straight into Delphie's. "Never forget that – always believe in it."

Delphie felt a longing to do the dance herself. She wanted to be up there, wanted Madame Za-Za to be watching her, but it was too late – it was the end of the class.

As soon as she had got changed, Delphie ran all the way home. She couldn't wait to tell her parents about it. This had been the best day of her life!

That night, when Delphie went to bed, she relived every moment of the class. *I'll have to learn the dance the others were doing*, she thought, picking up a book that was lying on her bedside table which told all the stories from the ballet.

Delphie turned to the chapter on *The Nutcracker*. She wanted to know what happened after Clara's dance. She read how, in the story, Clara dreams that the Nutcracker has come to life! Then the evil King Rat, with his army of mice, tries to fight the Nutcracker. Clara helps to defeat King Rat by throwing her slipper at his head, which knocks him out. Then the

Nutcracker changes into a handsome prince and takes Clara on a magical journey to the Land of Snow and the Land of Sweets. She meets the Sugar Plum Fairy and lots of other amazing characters like the snowflakes and Jack Frost, the Rose Fairy and the Arabian dancers.

Delphie sighed happily as she read the end of the story. Turning off the light she snuggled down in bed, imagining herself dancing Clara's dance, when suddenly she heard a faint tinkling sound and some faraway music. What was that?

She listened hard. There it was again. She sat up in bed.

The red ballet shoes were glittering and sparkling in the dark!

A Magical Land

Delphie stared at the twinkling shoes and then leapt out of bed. She was about to run out of the room to get her mum when Madame Za-Za' s voice came back to her: *They are special shoes, Delphie. I hope that one day you will find out just how special they are.*

Something seemed to be telling Delphie

to stay – not to go. She reached out and touched the shoes. Her fingers seemed to spark with a tiny electric shock and suddenly she felt as if she just had to put them on.

She picked up the left shoe. As she slipped it on, her foot felt light and sparkly. She put the other shoe on and as she tied the ribbons, the tingling spread through her whole body. Delphie stood up and then gasped as suddenly the shoes began to make her pirouette round and round...

Delphie whirled, her bedroom blurring into a sparkling haze of colours. She cried out. *What was happening?*

Then the colours faded and she found herself on a seat. She looked around in astonishment. She was in a large empty theatre. In front of her there was an enormous stage with red curtains, shut tight. The lights began to go down and before Delphie's eyes, the curtains rose.

A scene of a village street appeared with
a large mountain behind it. On the slope
of the mountain, a dark castle was painted.
Feeling sure that she must be dreaming,
Delphie looked at the stage. A fairy in a
pale lilac tutu was sitting on a tree stump,
her hands covering her face.

Behind her there were dancers dressed as multi-coloured flowers, two people in Russian costumes, a girl in a long red Spanish dress and a clown. Delphie wondered if this was the beginning of some sort of show, but as she looked more closely, she realised that the fairy was crying.

Delphie got to her feet and went down the aisle that led up to the stage. "Hello!" she called. Her voice sounded loud in the silence of the theatre.

The fairy jumped in surprise. "Who are you?"

"My name's Delphie," Delphie replied. "Who are you?"

"I'm the Sugar Plum Fairy," she said.

"You mean you're dancing the part of the Sugar Plum Fairy in *The Nutcracker*," Delphie said, feeling confused.

"No, I really am the Sugar Plum Fairy." The ballerina stood up, her sparkling tutu catching the lights on the stage. "People call me Sugar for short. This is the entrance to the Land of Enchantia – the land where the characters from all the different ballets live." She looked curiously at Delphie. "Where have you come from?"

"From… from my bedroom," Delphie stammered. "My ballet shoes started to sparkle and so I put them on and I ended up here."

"You've got the magic ballet shoes!" Sugar breathed. "I've heard about those.

Every so often they are given to someone who really loves ballet and they bring them to Enchantia. It happens whenever there's a problem here."

Delphie stared at her. "Madame Za-Za – the person who gave them to me – said they were special. She must have meant they were magic." Delphie's eyes widened and she looked around wonderingly. "So this is all real. It's not a dream." She remembered something the Sugar Plum Fairy had just said. "You said the shoes work when there's a problem."

Sugar nodded. "Yes, and we have a very big problem right now. The people in Enchantia usually live happily together and dance all day. But not any more." Her blue eyes welled up with tears. "Evil King Rat has stopped everyone from dancing."

"King Rat?" Delphie echoed, thinking back to the villain of the ballet she'd been reading about before she went to bed.

Sugar nodded sadly. "He hates dancing. He's captured the Nutcracker and turned him into a wooden toy. Without the magic of the Nutcracker no one in Enchantia can dance – all the toys have become lifeless, the sweets have become just sweets again and the snowflakes have frozen. I can't dance either. Look at this!"

49

She stood up and with a graceful lift of her arms, she rose on to her pointes but she only managed to dance three steps forwards before she wobbled over. "The magic of the dance has gone. The only way to stop King Rat is to free the Nutcracker and bring him back to life again but King Rat is keeping him prisoner in his castle and everyone's too scared to go there."

Delphie thought how awful it would be not to be able to dance. "I'll help you," she said eagerly.

"It could be very dangerous," Sugar warned. "The castle is guarded by King Rat's army of mice. They're big and carry swords and are very fierce."

"I don't care," said Delphie bravely. "I want to help you free the Nutcracker!"

"Oh, thank you!" Sugar grabbed Delphie's hands. "Thank you so much!"

"So, how do we get to the castle?" Delphie asked.

Sugar smiled. "By magic of course!"

Off to the Castle!

Sugar pulled a silver wand out of a pocket in her tutu and waved it in the air. Purple sparks flew out and swirled round them in a haze. Delphie felt herself pirouetting round three times in the air before she landed on her feet and the sparkles cleared.

Delphie gasped. They were no longer on the stage but standing in a wood with fallen branches and leaves beneath their feet. The air smelt horrid – of rotten fruit and old food.

"That's King Rat's castle," whispered Sugar pointing through the trees. Delphie could see a dark shape looming ahead of them, its stone turrets silhouetted against the sky.

Two mice, a bit taller than Delphie, were guarding the big wooden door that led into the castle. They were standing on their back legs and had swords slung through leather belts. Their eyes were beady and their snouts were long.

"What's that horrid smell?" Delphie whispered back.

"King Rat gets his mice to bring great piles of rubbish here so he can rummage around in it and eat it to his heart's content. He loves it."

Sugar waved her wand. There was a tinkle of music and two sugar-coated plums appeared in her hand. "These should help take the smell away. Put one in your pocket." She handed one to Delphie.

Delphie breathed in a wave of sweetness – icing sugar, candyfloss, fresh plums and peaches. "That's much

better!" She slipped the sugarplum into her pocket and looked around. "How are we going to get into the castle to rescue the Nutcracker?"

"I don't know," said Sugar. "I can use my magic to travel around Enchantia, but I can't use it to get inside King Rat's castle. His powers are much stronger than mine."

Delphie crept forward to the edge of the trees. How were they going to get in?

Suddenly both mice sniffed the air.

"Sugarplums!" said the mouse on the left who was tall and thin with very pointed teeth. "I smell sugarplums!"

"Me too," said the other mouse, who was smaller and fatter with tiny eyes.

They scented the air. "It smells like they're this way!" said the thin mouse, starting to walk away from the castle and towards the trees where Delphie and Sugar were hiding.

"They're coming over here!" Delphie whispered in alarm.

Sugar looked dismayed. "I forgot that all of King Rat's mice love sugarplums! I'd better magic us away!"

But Delphie had noticed something. With the mice walking away from the castle, the door was unguarded. An idea popped into her mind. If they could just get the mice into the trees and properly away from the door...

"Wait!" she hissed as Sugar lifted her wand. "This could be our chance to get into the castle! Can you get me some more sugarplums – and fast!"

"It's too dangerous!" said Sugar as the mice approached the trees.

"Please!" Delphie begged.

Sugar hesitated and then pointed her wand at the ground. With a faint tinkle, a pile of sugarplums appeared.

Delphie picked up as many as she could. "Quick! Let's make a trail leading away from the castle!"

Sugar grabbed the remaining plums and they hurried through the trees. They placed one of the plums near the entrance to the wood and then another and then another, all leading down the hill away from the castle. Delphie glanced round. Already she could hear the mice crashing through the woods! Sugar put the last plum where the wood ended in a steep bank that led into a shallow but fast-flowing stream.

Delphie suddenly had an idea of how to get the mice really out of the way. "If only we had some string."

"How about some ballet ribbon!" Sugar waved her wand and a big roll of pink ribbon appeared in her hand. "What do you want it for?"

"To hopefully get two mice very wet!" grinned Delphie.

She raced to the bank and tied one end of the ribbon round a tree on the left side

 and the other end round a tree on the right side. Then she smiled and grabbed Sugar's hand. "Come on! They mustn't see us."

She pulled Sugar back to the edge of the
woods where there was a big bramble bush
to hide behind, just as the smaller mouse
burst into sight.

"I found the sugarplum!" he exclaimed,
snatching it up.

The tall one appeared just behind him.
"There's another!" he cried, pouncing on
the pale fruit. "And look! There's more of
them!"

Peeping out from behind the bush, Delphie and Sugar watched as the mice began to run down the hill, scooping up the sweet plums and squabbling over them.

"I saw that one first!"

"I want it!"

"No! I want it!"

The two mice were so busy jostling and pushing each other that they didn't see the ribbon stretched across the path until they both tripped over it.

"Whoa!" shouted the mice grabbing hold of each other as they crashed to the ground. Over and over they tumbled down the bank until with two very loud splashes they fell, still shouting, into the stream.

Sugar gasped, looking half-shocked and half-delighted. "Oh, Delphie! You've made them so wet!"

Delphie grinned. "Maybe that'll teach them not to be so greedy in future. Come on! Let's get inside the castle while they're busy drying off."

They raced towards the entrance. The wooden door had a huge metal handle in the shape of a rat's head. Delphie turned it and the door opened. On the other side there was an enormous empty hall with a stone fireplace. Above it there was a framed picture of a black rat with a crown on his head and a red cloak.

On the far side of the room were two towers of boxes, piled almost up to the ceiling with the words GLUE printed on the sides of them.

"Look!" Sugar pointed to a table just in front of the boxes. Standing on top of it was a small painted wooden figure. He looked like a soldier wearing a red jacket with brass buttons, black trousers and boots and a sword in his belt.

"It's the Nutcracker!" Delphie said, running over and picking the figure up.

But then she heard a noise. It sounded like footsteps marching towards the door on the left.

"Get back in the hall!" came a voice outside the door. "You know King Rat said the Nutcracker wasn't to be left on his own! Call yourself a soldier! Coming to me with poppycock stories about smelling sugarplums through the windows!"

"But I did, Sarge. I really did. I…"

"GET BACK IN THERE!"

"Quick!" Delphie gasped to Sugar. "There's someone coming! We've got to hide!"

Dancing Magic

Delphie ran over and turned the handle of a door at the side of the hall. It opened into a small room which seemed to be used for keeping firewood. "In here!" she gasped.

Just as they were about to go in, Sugar waved her wand at the table. There was a tinkling sound and she magicked up another Nutcracker doll. "I'll put this on the table in front of the boxes so that they won't realise the real nutcracker has gone."

Delphie and Sugar dived into the room and peeped back round the door just in time. Two mice hurried into the hall. One was dressed with boots and a sword like the mice outside had been. The other was wearing a smart waistcoat with gold buttons. He looked very relieved when he saw the fake Nutcracker on the table in front of the boxes. "Lucky for you that the Nutcracker's still here. King Rat's been ever so pleased since he turned him into a toy.

He was going to use the quick-drying glue in those boxes to stick all those horrible dancers to the ground but he doesn't have to now. No

one can dance while the Nutcracker's a prisoner here." He glowered at the other mouse. "So, stay where you are and don't let anyone past!"

The other mouse nodded and the Sergeant strode out.

Sugar looked scared. "If that mouse stays outside the door then we're trapped in here!"

"Maybe there's another way out." Delphie looked around. But there were no windows or other doors in the little room.

"If only we could bring the Nutcracker back to life, he would be able to help us fight our way out," Sugar said.

"Can't you use your magic to make him come alive again?" Delphie asked hopefully.

Sugar shook her head. "King Rat's

powers are too strong while we're inside the castle. Only really powerful magic will turn him back."

Suddenly Delphie heard Madame Za-Za's words from that afternoon echo in her head: *The real magic of the ballet comes from telling a story and making the audience believe in that story. Never forget that – always believe in it.*

Delphie remembered how Madame Za-Za had looked straight at her while she had been speaking. It had been as if she had been talking directly to her. *Never forget the story...*

Maybe she'd been trying to tell her something. Delphie began to think hard. What happened in the story of *The Nutcracker* before the toy came to life?

Of course, she realised. *Clara dances with the toy Nutcracker.* An idea grew in her head. Maybe if she danced with *this* Nutcracker he would come to life too!

Almost before the idea had formed in her mind, Delphie's feet began to tingle and in her head she heard the opening bars of the dance she had watched the girls doing that afternoon. Delphie moved forward into the opening pose. Holding her arms down low and with her left foot pointed forward in front of her, she looked down at the Nutcracker in her hands.

I'm Clara, she told herself and then she began to do the dance she had been longing to do ever since the class that afternoon.

She skipped forward with tiny steps as if she was floating across the floor. Stopping, she raised her hands, drew her right leg up against her left and stretched it out behind her, staying perfectly balanced.

She gasped. The Nutcracker's arm had started to raise and his mouth to open…

Sugar stared. "Your dance is bringing him to life! Dance some more, Delphie!"

Delphie didn't need any more urging. She moved into a pirouette, ran forward a few steps then nimbly jumped into the air. She lifted the Nutcracker high up and spun round with him, her whole body glowing and tingling with the music as in her mind she became Clara dancing with her beloved doll.

There was a bright white flash. Delphie stopped with a gasp. The Nutcracker had come to life!

"Hello, Delphie," he said, smiling down at her.

Sugar threw her arms around him. "Oh, Nutcracker! Delphie's brought you back by dancing."

The Nutcracker nodded. "The strongest magic of all." He hugged her. "And now everyone in Enchantia will be able to dance again!" He looked at Delphie. "I can't thank you enough. You must have really believed in the dance to make the magic work." He took her hand. "Thank you," he said softly.

Delphie grinned in delight.

Sugar ran to the door. "We need to get out of here then I can use my magic to take us back to the village.

"Follow me!" The Nutcracker pulled out his sword and opened the door.

Escape!

The mouse who was standing guard by the table squeaked in surprise. "It's you!" He swung round and looked at the fake Nutcracker doll. "But... but... how can it be?"

The Nutcracker smiled. "Ballet magic," he said. "Let us past!"

"Oh no you don't," said the mouse running

to stand between him and the front door.
"You aren't getting away that easily!"

With one swift movement the Nutcracker
danced forward and used his sword to flip
the sword out of the mouse's grip. It flew
into the air and landed with a clatter on the
floor. With nothing to protect him, the
mouse ran hastily backwards. "Help!
Help!" he shouted. "The Nutcracker's
escaping!"

There was the sound of running footsteps.
Then suddenly a door slammed open and a
very loud voice boomed into the room.

"What is the meaning of this?"

The mice cringed, and Delphie stared as a
haughty black rat with red eyes walked
into the room, flanked by four guards.

He was wearing a
purple cloak
trimmed with
white fur, and
he had a
golden crown
on his head.
He saw the
Nutcracker
and stopped.
"You!" he
exclaimed. "I
turned you into
a toy!"

"But now I have turned back!" cried the
Nutcracker. "And all of Enchantia will
dance again!"

"Not if I have anything to do with it!" King Rat leapt forward, swiping his sword viciously at the Nutcracker. His guards closed in as well. Bravely, the Nutcracker fought them off with strong, sweeping swipes. But he was being beaten back.

"There's too many of them for the Nutcracker to fight!" Sugar exclaimed as the king and the guards advanced with their swords. They began to back the brave Nutcracker into the corner where the piles of boxes marked GLUE were stacked. He knocked against them and they wobbled precariously.

Suddenly, Delphie had an idea. She pulled off one of her ballet shoes. "Stop it, King Rat!" she shouted.

King Rat swung round. "Who are you?"

"Delphie!" She lifted the shoe up and hurled it at him.

King Rat ducked. "That's the oldest trick in the book!" he said as the shoe hit the boxes behind him. "Missed!"

"Oh no I didn't!" exclaimed Delphie as the pile of boxes began to sway.

The Nutcracker leapt nimbly out of the way, grabbing Delphie's ballet shoe from the floor as he did so, but King Rat was too busy laughing at Delphie to notice the boxes. "You missed! You did! You…"

His voice was drowned out as the boxes toppled over. They crashed down, jars of glue raining on his head. "Ow! Ooh! Ow!" he yelled.

The guards cried and shouted too. The jars smashed into each other as they fell, cracking open and covering King Rat and his soldiers in quick-drying white glue.

King Rat pointed at Delphie, glue dripping down over his face and off his ears and whiskers. "Why you… you…!"

But though he tried to run towards her, his feet were stuck fast!

"Come on," gasped Delphie, turning to Sugar and the Nutcracker. "Let's get out of here!"

And quickly they raced out of the castle and back to the woods.

"That was brilliant, Delphie!" exclaimed Sugar.

"Fantastic!" said the Nutcracker, giving her her shoe back.

"We're free – that's the main thing," Delphie grinned as she put it back on.

"And Enchantia should be returned to normal," said Sugar. "Come on, let's use my magic to get away from here and see what's happening!"

She waved her wand. Delphie found herself spinning round three times. When they landed she saw that they were in the village that she had seen painted on the scenery in the theatre. The streets were full of characters from the ballet – toys, enormous sweets, dancers dressed up

as bright flowers, two Spanish dancers and
a beautiful fairy in a rose-pink dress
dancing on her pointes.

Music was flooding magically through
the air. Sugar grabbed Delphie's hands.
"Let's dance!"

Holding lightly on to the Sugar Plum
Fairy's hands, Delphie felt herself being
swept up in the music – she didn't have to
stop to think what steps she was going to
do. As Sugar rose on to her pointes, Delphie
let the music guide her – she skimmed
across the ground with tiny steps, and
jumped into the air, her arms outstretched,
her toes pointed. She landed softly and then,
with perfect balance, she stretched one leg
out behind her. Delphie couldn't believe

how graceful she felt! It seemed like the music
was flowing through her as she and Sugar
ran forward together and pirouetted. The
Nutcracker leapt in front of them, turning
into a handsome prince as he landed. His

glittering costume perfectly matched Sugar's. Delphie gasped as he swept the Sugar Plum Fairy up in his arms and lifted her high into the air. He turned and placed her lightly down. Holding on to his hand she turned round on the tip of her toe. All around them the other characters danced too – the flowers waltzed, the snowflakes twirled, the Spanish dancers swung their tiered red skirts and the Russian dancers linked arms. There was colour and movement everywhere. The Nutcracker and Sugar came to a stop, their cheeks flushed, their eyes shining.

"It is almost time for you to go home, Delphie," the Nutcracker Prince said. "We can't thank you enough."

A thought struck Delphie. "I hope Mum and Dad don't wonder where I've gone!"

"Do not worry, time is different in our world and yours," said the Nutcracker. "When you get back you will find that it will be as if no time has passed at all."

Delphie felt relieved but also sad as she looked around at the enchanted world. "I don't want to leave here."

Sugar smiled at her. "You'll come back. You have the magic ballet shoes. Whenever we need you they will sparkle. If you put them on they will bring you to Enchantia again." She danced over and kissed Delphie on both cheeks, then she took out her wand. "This is to take home to remind you of us," she said, waving sparkles in the air.

Delphie gasped as a beautiful white tutu appeared in her hand. "Goodbye – and thank you," Sugar said. "Send my regards to Madame Za-Za." And with that she waved her wand over Delphie's head.

"Goodbye!" Delphie cried as the air around her swirled with colour and she began to pirouette round and round… till suddenly, she landed with a bump…

Home Again

She was back in her bedroom sitting on her bed with a beautiful white tutu lying next to her.

Could her mother have put it there?

"Perhaps it was real after all," she whispered, her head spinning as she thought about everything that had just happened. She looked down at the ballet

shoes on her feet and remembered Madame Za-Za's words: *They are very special shoes, Delphie. I hope one day you find out just how special they are...*

Delphie could hardly believe it. As she began to unlace the ribbons she thought about her ballet lessons. After her adventures in Enchantia, she was even more determined to practise really hard and get as good at ballet as she could. *After all, the better I am, the more I should be able to help in Enchantia,* she realised.

Delphie stood up and put the tutu and the shoes carefully on her bedside table. When would she next go to Enchantia and what would she have to do? She remembered what the Sugar Plum Fairy

had said: *You have the magic ballet shoes.*
Whenever we need you they will sparkle and
if you put them on they will bring you to
Enchantia.

Delphie hugged her arms around herself.
She might not know when it was going to
happen or for what she might be needed
but if the shoes glowed again, she would be
there to help in whatever way she could!

*Tiptoe over the page to learn
a special dance step...*

Darcey's Magical Masterclass

Ballet Positions

Now it's your turn. Have fun!

Prepare
Put your heels together with toes pointing outwards. Make an oval shape with your arms.

First position
Now move your arms upwards so that your hands are in line with your belly button.

Second Position
Move your feet to
hips-width apart,
and open your arms.

Third position
Move your right foot
so that the heel touches the
middle of your left foot; Sweep
your left arm in front of you.

Fourth position
Slide your right foot forwards
and lift your left arm so it is
almost over your head.

Fifth position
Now bring both your
arms over your head.

Magic Ballerina
Delphie and the Magic Spell

King Rat is up to his old tricks and has
cast a spell over all of Enchantia; can
Delphie help her friends before it's too late?

**Read on for a sneak preview
of Delphie and the Magic Spell . . .**

°ⓞ`*`☆ⓞ`*`☆ⓞ`*`☆ⓞ`*`°

Delphie landed with a bump to find herself in the same darkened theatre only this time the air was very cold. She jumped up eagerly and then caught her breath. It was all so different. The first time she had been here there had been light and colour. The scenery had shown mountains, fields and a village, as well as King Rat's castle, and there had been lots of characters on the stage even though they had all been asleep.

But now the background scenery was just painted white and the stage was empty. The floor was covered in a thick blanket of snow. There were bare trees on the stage, their branches covered in icicles.

Delphie walked hesitantly towards the stage. "Sugar?" Her voice echoed through the empty theatre. She didn't like this. There was a feeling in the air as if something was horribly wrong.

"Sugar!" she called uneasily. "Where are you?…"

Magic Ballerina

Rosa and the Secret Princess

Darcey Bussell

To Phoebe and Zoe, as they are the inspiration behind Magic Ballerina.

Contents

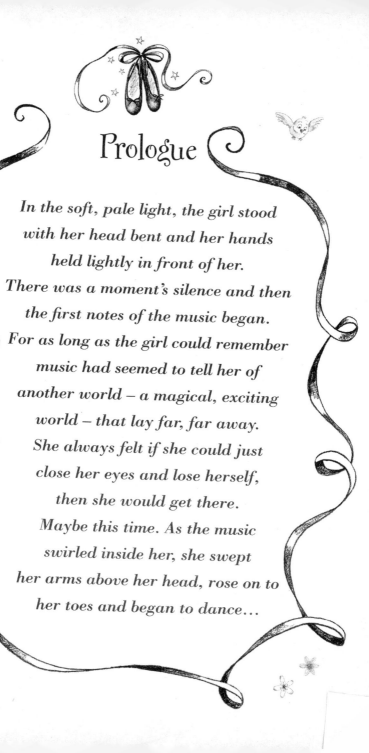

Prologue

In the soft, pale light, the girl stood
with her head bent and her hands
held lightly in front of her.
There was a moment's silence and then
the first notes of the music began.
For as long as the girl could remember
music had seemed to tell her of
another world – a magical, exciting
world – that lay far, far away.
She always felt if she could just
close her eyes and lose herself,
then she would get there.
Maybe this time. As the music
swirled inside her, she swept
her arms above her head, rose on to
her toes and began to dance…

Rosa

Rosa ran up the steps to the old front door and turned the brass handle. She liked to get to Madame Za-Za's ballet school early so she could warm up before class and today was particularly special because it was her first day back after the summer holidays. She couldn't wait for classes to start again.

Hurrying to the changing rooms, she put on her pink leotard. Over the summer she had made a new friend, Olivia, who was going to be starting at the ballet school that very day. Rosa had arranged to meet her before class to show her around. She was really looking forward to it!

It's going to be very different this term, she thought. Several of the older girls who had been in her class had moved up into another group. Rosa was going to miss them, particularly her friend, Delphie. At the end of last term, Delphie had given Rosa a pair of red ballet shoes that didn't fit her any longer. They were very old and the leather was very soft. Now Rosa took them out of her bag and put them on, crossing the ribbons neatly over

her ankles and tying them firmly. They fitted perfectly.

When Delphie had given her the shoes, she had said something odd – something about:

"Watch out for King Rat".

Rosa didn't have a clue what she had meant by that, and the few times she had seen Delphie in the summer, the dark-haired girl had refused to tell her. She had just kept smiling mysteriously and saying that the ballet shoes were very special.

And indeed, Rosa loved them and couldn't

107

wait to start dancing. Going over to the mirror, she fixed her long white-blonde hair into a bun. Then she put on her favourite hairclip before leaving the changing rooms to go to the ballet studio. She wished she could come to classes every day. *When I'm older I will,* she thought. She was determined she was going to be a ballerina just like her mum had once been. Her mother didn't dance any more because she had been in a car accident, which had left her in a wheelchair, but she helped Rosa practise.

Rosa went to the long wooden *barre* that ran all the way around the walls and began to warm up. The red ballet shoes felt really comfortable, and it was so lovely to be back in the ballet studio again that she completely

lost track of the time. A little while later she looked at the clock and gasped. It was only a few minutes until the class started. She had promised Olivia she would meet her in the changing rooms almost ten minutes ago!

As Rosa ran back to the changing rooms, she was worried that Olivia would be alone and upset. She burst through the changing room doors and stopped dead…

Olivia was standing there with two of the other girls from the class. She was laughing as one of them helped her tie her brown hair back and smiled, in what seemed to Rosa a casual way. "Oh, hi there, Rosa!"

"Hi. I'm… I'm sorry I wasn't here to meet you," Rosa said, feeling a bit silly to have burst in so quickly. She felt suddenly unsure of herself, seeing her friend so at ease.

Olivia smiled. "Don't worry. Everyone's been really friendly. Asha and Rebecca showed me round."

Asha, who was fixing Olivia's hair, smiled.

"Madame Za-Za's a cool teacher. I bet you're going to love coming to classes here, Olivia."

A mixture of emotions swirled around inside Rosa. She was pleased that Olivia wasn't upset but she also felt a tiny twinge of jealousy that the other girls had been the ones to take her new friend around. "I was going to show you how it worked and help you get ready," she said. She knew she sounded cross and grumpy but she couldn't stop herself. Olivia looked surprised. "But you weren't here, Rosa and…" She broke off. "Look, why don't you show me round again after class?"

"Oh, what's the point?" Rosa said angrily. "You've seen everything now!" And with that, she marched back to the ballet studio.

Magic!

As soon as Rosa got to the studio, her anger faded. She felt awful. She shouldn't have snapped like that. All Olivia had done was make friends with the others.

I'd better say sorry, Rosa thought guiltily. She felt annoyed with herself. Her mum was always telling her she needed to control her temper and think more before she acted but sometimes she just couldn't help herself. It just welled up inside her and came out – like all the times in her old school when the girls had teased her about her mum. Just then, Olivia came into the studio with the other girls and gave her a hurt look. But before Rosa could run over and apologise, Madame Za-Za also came in. The ballet teacher was wearing a calf-length dress and bangles on her wrists. Her hair was tied back in a loose bun. Her face was lined but her eyes were very bright. She clapped her hands for silence.

"Welcome, girls. Let's start at the *barre*. No talking please!"

Rosa knew there would be no chance to say sorry now until the end of the class. Madame Za-Za got very cross if she thought anyone was chatting and not listening. "Facing the *barre*, first position please."

Rosa followed Madame Za-Za's instructions wishing she could apologise.

After they had worked at the *barre* and then in the centre of the room, Madame Za-Za told them that they were going to learn a dance from *Swan Lake*.

"Who can tell me the story of *Swan Lake*?" she asked.

Rosa put up her hand. It had been the last ballet her mother had ever danced in and one of her favourites. "It's about a magician who enchants a princess called Odette. In the

day time she's a swan – the Swan Queen –
but at night time she turns back into a girl."

"Very good," said Madame Za-Za. "That is
indeed the basis of the story. One night, a
prince sees the Swan Queen, falls in love
with her and invites her to a ball. But the evil
magician stops Odette from going and
instead uses magic to disguise his daughter,
Odile, to look like her. The prince thinking
Odile is Odette asks her to marry him."

Madame Za-Za smiled. "You will all be
swans dancing with the Swan Queen. Rosa, I
would like you to be the main part."

Rosa gasped. "Me!"

Madame Za-Za smiled at her. "I am sure
you will dance it very well."

Rosa was delighted. She listened intently

to Madame Za-Za's instructions as all
the swans surrounded the Swan Queen.

There was one tricky bit where she had to
dance to one side and then the other, before
turning another pirouette while the others
danced in towards her and then out, over
and over again. They practised it quite a few

times without the music and then Madame
Za-Za put the CD on. Rosa really wanted to
get it right. But she overbalanced on her
pirouette and bumped into Olivia, treading
heavily on her foot. Olivia gasped and
stumbled into Asha, knocking her over.

Madame Za-Za snapped the music off. "Honestly, girls. Come along, you can do better than that! Up you get, Asha. Let's try again."

Rosa looked quickly at Olivia. She tried to mouth "sorry" but Olivia turned away. Rosa groaned inwardly. She was sure Olivia thought she had stood on her foot on purpose.

When the class finished, she hurried towards her friend.

"Rosa!" Madame Za-Za called. "May I have a word please?"

Rosa shot a look at Olivia's disappearing back but there was nothing she could do. She walked back to the teacher. Madame Za-Za was putting away the CD. Rosa waited as she finished.

"I see you have the red ballet shoes, Rosa,"
Madame Za-Za said.

Rosa nodded. "Delphie Durand gave them
to me."

Madame Za-Za smiled. "So they found the
perfect home. Did you know they used to
belong to me a long time ago?"

"No," Rosa said, in her astonishment
forgetting about Olivia.

Madame Za-Za nodded. "They are very
special shoes, Rosa."

Rosa and the Secret Princess

"Delphie told me that," Rosa said.

"I hope you find out quite how special they are," Madame Za-Za smiled warmly. "Now, go and get changed."

Part of Rosa wanted to ask Madame Za-Za what she meant about the shoes being special but she also wanted to catch Olivia before she left. She hurried out but saw it was too late. Olivia was just going through the front door with her mother.

"Olivia!" Rosa called.

But Olivia had already walked out and the door was shutting behind her.

Rosa's heart sank. *I'll phone her and say sorry as soon as I get home,* she thought as she went to the changing room.

The other girls were just leaving. They

121

called goodbye and soon Rosa was on her own. She sat down and bent over to untie the ribbons on her red shoes. As she did so her feet started to tingle. She gasped. The shoes were sparkling and glowing!

She jumped to her feet and then cried out in astonishment as a swirl of rainbow colours and a sweet tinkling of music surrounded her. She started to spin round!

What was going on? She shut her eyes tightly, her heart pounding. Round and round she went until her feet met solid ground. She blinked.

She wasn't in the changing rooms any more, she was standing in a forest, and through the trees she could see a shimmering dark lake with a single swan swimming on it!

The Swan Princess

Rosa stared. Where was she? No wonder Delphie and Madame Za-Za had been telling her the ballet shoes were special! *They're magic*, she thought, her heart flipping. *Oh wow!*

There were tall trees all around her and to the right of the lake she could see a big, dark castle. What should she do? She couldn't just

stay standing there. Which way should she go?

Not to the castle, she decided. It looked so forbidding. Instead, she made her way cautiously through the trees towards the lake.

Suddenly, she saw a flash of pink ahead of her. There was someone dancing in the trees. She hurried forward and stopped in amazement as she saw that the dancer was a fairy! The fairy had a tutu made of layers of brown and pink silk and a pale pink bodice with sequins embroidered over it. Her wavy chestnut hair was tied back in a bun. She had delicate wings and in one hand she held a wand. As she saw Rosa, she stopped with a gasp. Her gaze flew to Rosa's feet. "You're

the girl with the red shoes! The new girl!"
She ran over, her brown eyes shining with
excitement. "Oh, I'm so glad to see you!"

"You are?" Rosa said in bewilderment.

"Of course!" The fairy seized her hands.
"You're here to help, aren't you? Sugar told
me you would come."

"Help?" echoed Rosa. "Who's Sugar? And where exactly am I?"

"You're in Enchantia, of course!" said the fairy breathlessly. "The magical land of ballet. Oh dear, I'm sorry," she said, looking at Rosa's bewildered face. "Sugar said you wouldn't have been here before and that I had to tell you everything from the beginning. It's just I'm so excited to see you. I haven't been doing proper magic for very long and I've never met a human before!"

Rosa smiled cautiously as the fairy's words tumbled out one after another. "So who exactly is Sugar?" she asked.

The fairy took a deep breath and spoke a little more slowly. "She's my older sister – the Sugar Plum Fairy - she knows lots about magic. I'm Nutmeg by the way. Whenever we have a big problem in Enchantia the red ballet shoes bring someone from your world who can help us, a girl who loves to dance."

Rosa stared at her. So she was in a magic land and she was there to help!

"Will… will I get to go home again?" she asked.

Nutmeg nodded. "Of course. The shoes will take you back when the problem is solved. No time passes in the human world while you're here so no one will even know you've been gone."

Rosa breathed a sigh of relief. For a

moment she had thought about her mum waiting for her and getting really worried. That would have been dreadful!

"What's your name?" the fairy asked.

"Rosa."

"It's so lovely to see you, Rosa. We really need your help," Nutmeg said. "King Rat's causing dreadful trouble again!"

"King Rat!" Rosa breathed, remembering Delphie's words. So *that* must have been what Delphie was talking about. She must have come here too!

"Yes," replied Nutmeg. "You see everyone in Enchantia loves dancing except for that horrible rodent. He keeps coming up with mean plans to stop us and now he's taken the King and Queen's niece, Princess Cressida."

"Princess Cressida?" Rosa scratched her head. It was all a lot to take in.

"Yes, Cressida was on her way to visit her aunt and uncle to keep them company whilst their own daughter, Aurelia, is away. Nutmeg explained. Anyway, King Rat has captured Cressida to stop all the balls and dancing that would go on for her visit. Without her at the palace there won't be any celebrations."

"So where has he taken her?" breathed Rosa.

"She's here in his castle grounds," said Nutmeg. "He's put a spell on her so that by day she's a swan, but by night she's the princess again."

"Just like *Swan Lake*!" Rosa said excitedly.

"Yes, exactly," Nutmeg nodded. "That's where King Rat got the idea from. Look,

there's Princess Cressida on the Enchanted Lake now." Nutmeg pointed towards the graceful white swan on the shimmering water. "Sugar has asked me to stand guard to check that King Rat doesn't whisk her away somewhere else or put even more spells on

her, but she doesn't even realise I'm here. You see she forgets all about being a princess in the day. It just comes back to her as the

sun sets and she flies back to her room in the castle's towers and turns back into her old self."

"Oh, the poor thing," Rosa said, her heart going out to the princess.

Nutmeg shivered. "Everyone in Enchantia keeps trying to think up a plan to rescue her, but we haven't come up with anything yet. If only we could get her out of King Rat's castle grounds, the enchantment would be broken. But the lake is enchanted so we can't swim

or row across to get her and she wouldn't recognise us anyway."

Rosa thought for a moment. "Can't you use magic to rescue her at night when she's locked inside?"

Nutmeg shook her head. "King Rat's magic is much too powerful. He's put spells on the castle so that no one else can do strong magic either in it or its grounds. I stay in the trees because some of my magic still works in the forest. Also, I can keep watch on Cressida and magic myself away if his horrible scary guards come." She clasped her hands together. "Oh, Rosa. Can *you* think of a way we could rescue the princess?"

Rosa stared at her helplessly and gulped. It all seemed pretty impossible. "I wish I could," she said. "But I really haven't got any other ideas."

"Then Princess Cressida will just have to stay a secret princess forever!" exclaimed Nutmeg, her eyes filling with tears.

"Look, we can't give up that easily!" Rosa declared. "Hmm, what could we do?" She glanced around. "You know, maybe we don't need magic to get us into the castle. Maybe we could just sneak inside. We could hide somewhere until the princess comes back then let her out of her room and all escape together!"

"But that would be really dangerous!" said Nutmeg. "King Rat's guards are very fierce!" She caught her breath. "Here they come now!"

A group of ten mice came swaggering around the side of the castle. Rosa stared. They were walking on their back legs and were way taller than her, with pointed teeth and long swords hanging from their belts.

They stopped. A couple of them leaned against the castle walls, the others mooched  about. They looked fed up.

"I'm bored of marching round the castle," one of them grumbled.

"Me too," said another. "My paws are hurting. King Rat's out at the moment so

Magic Ballerina

why don't we go and have a sit down?"

"Yeah!" said the first mouse. "If we go round to the other side of the castle we can listen out for King Rat coming back and when he gets here just start marching again." He looked around at the others. "What do you reckon?"

They all nodded. "Good plan!"

"What about the Sergeant?" said one. "If he sees us he'll go mad."

The first mouse shrugged. "He's inside somewhere. Probably in the kitchens stuffing his face. I bet he'll never notice. Come on!"

They all ambled off around the side of the castle.

Nutmeg shivered. "They're horrible!"

But Rosa's mind was racing with what the

136

mice had just said. "Did you hear what they were talking about? King Rat's out and they are going to take a break. Oh, Nutmeg! Why don't we try to get into the castle right now?"

"But it's daytime and Cressida is on the lake."

"So? We can hide somewhere inside until the sun sets and she comes back. It's the perfect opportunity. Come on! Let's see if there's a door or window open."

Rosa started to hurry through the trees towards the castle.

"Wait, Rosa!" exclaimed Nutmeg, flying after her. "It's too dangerous! The guards might change their minds and come back."

"Then we'd better be as quick as possible," said Rosa. "It's now or never!"

"No! I don't think we should," Nutmeg insisted. "Look, let's just stay here for a little while longer and see if we can think of another plan. Come on! I'm going back to the lake."

She flew back towards the lake. Rosa hesitated. She thought of the poor secret princess. She *had* to help her! Surely getting into the castle was the only way and while the guards were taking a break it was the

perfect opportunity! *I'm going to try and get in whether Nutmeg wants to come or not,* she decided impulsively. And she began to hurry through the trees.

Captured!

Rosa's eyes scanned the castle, but the only
windows that were open were right up at the
top of the tower. There was a small door to
the right of the main entrance. Maybe that
would be unlocked?

A short stretch of grass separated the
wood and the castle. She took a deep breath
and ran across it. Reaching the small door,

she turned the handle… locked! Suddenly she heard a sharp voice from around the side of the castle…

"I can't believe you lot. Get back to patrolling the castle right now! Lying around! Lazing about! Honestly. I can't trust you for a second! If King Rat catches you he'll have your guts for garters. Come on! Hup two, hup two!"

There was the sound of general mumbling and grumbling and the stamp of boots heading towards the front of the castle.

Rosa froze to the spot. The guards were coming! She looked round desperately. Where could she hide? There were some giant pots that looked like they had once had plants in them.

Rosa raced to the nearest one and scrambled inside. The bottom was covered with old dry soil and as she landed, it blew up in clouds around her. She could feel a sneeze tickling in her nose…

She covered her face with her hands as the grumbling guards came around the side of

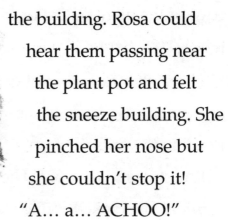 the building. Rosa could hear them passing near the plant pot and felt the sneeze building. She pinched her nose but she couldn't stop it!

"A… a… ACHOO!"

"What was that?" the leader's voice snapped out.

The guards' footsteps stopped.

"There's someone hiding!" said the Sergeant. "Find them!"

Rosa huddled down in the bottom of the plant pot, her heart beating painfully against her ribcage. *Please don't look in here,* she thought as footsteps echoed around her...

Too late... A pointed face peered over the edge of the plant pot before shrieking out loudly. "Oi, Sarge! I've found someone! I've found someone!"

"Get them out then, Mangy Tail!"

The flowerpot was tipped over roughly and Rosa tumbled out. She scrambled to her feet, scared, dusty and dishevelled.

"Who are you?" the Sergeant demanded.

"N… no one!" Rosa stammered.

"I bet she's trying to help that silly princess, Sarge," said the mouse. "I bet she's a spy!"

The Sergeant nodded. "Take her to the dungeons!"

"No!" gasped Rosa. But Mangy Tail and another mouse took her by the arms. They were very strong and although she kicked and struggled they had no problem holding on to her.

"Stop your wriggling, Prisoner!" snarled

the Sergeant, poking her with the hilt of his sword.

Hastily Rosa did as she was told. She was dragged into the castle and through a big entrance hall before being pushed down a long flight of stairs. The Sergeant clambered round her and opened a heavy door ahead. "In there!" he ordered.

He pushed Rosa hard through the doorway. She fell over and heard a bolt being pushed firmly across the door on the other side.

"You'll stay there until we tell King Rat about you!" snapped the Sergeant through the door. "Mangy Tail and Whiskers, you guard her."

"Yes, Sarge!" said two eager voices.

Rosa's heart sank at the sound of heavy feet traipsing away and the two guards talking in low voices outside the door.

She shivered as she looked around her. The room was very small with no windows.

Rosa bit her lip. How could she have been silly enough to think she could get into the castle so easily? She was trapped!

And what about King Rat? What would he do to her? And how would Nutmeg feel when she realised Rosa was missing? If the fairy had seen her being captured she would be so worried. Rosa felt awful. She had let her new friend down. There she'd gone again, just charging in without thinking.

I should never have headed off like that, she thought in despair. *I've just made it all worse.*

She looked at her shoes, hoping they might sparkle and whisk her away somewhere, but nothing happened. And Nutmeg couldn't rescue her by magic because she had told Rosa that her magic didn't work in the castle. *If I'm going to get out of here, I'm going to have to get myself out*, Rosa realised.

She thought hard. There were guards on the other side of the door but only two.

She went to the door and banged on it.

"Shut up!" snarled a mouse's voice from

the other side of the door.

"If you want food, there isn't any," said a higher pitched voice.

Mangy Tail, thought Rosa recognising the guard's voice from earlier.

"I don't want food," she said. "I don't feel very well." She started to make sounds as if  she was about to be sick as loud as she could.

"Yuck!" she heard Whiskers exclaim. "If she's sick in there I bet we'll have to clear it up!"

"I just need some fresh air," said Rosa, acting for all she was worth. "I'm sure I'll be fine then but if I don't get some fresh air I think I'll be sick EVERYWHERE!"

"Come on, come on, let her out," said Mangy Tail hurriedly.

Rosa heard the sound of the bolt sliding back and saw the door starting to open. She leaped to one side and crouched down in the shadows, staying as still as possible till the mice stepped into the doorway.

"Where are you?" Whiskers demanded, looking round.

Rosa leaped up, yelling as loudly as she could and the two mice jumped in alarm. Then Rosa charged at them, waving her hands about. It wasn't exactly a well-thought-out plan but hopefully it would do!

"Whoa!" Whiskers yelled, staggering into Mangy Tail and knocking him over. Rosa

leaped lightly over Mangy Tail's fallen body, landing in perfect balance, before pushing Whiskers with all her might. He tripped over Mangy Tail, and they both rolled into the room.

Rosa slammed the door shut and pushed the bolt across, her fingers trembling. She'd done it! She'd escaped!

The mice started banging on the door and shouting but it was a very thick door and the noise was muffled.

I'm free! Rosa thought. She raced up the stairs. No one was in the main hall. The front door was just opposite her. But just as she was about to make her escape, she saw the big door handle turn and heard a loud voice...

"So the prisoner's a girl, you say? A girl with red ballet shoes? But not the same girl who has been to Enchantia before?"

"A different one, King Rat. Definitely a different one."

Rosa ran through a nearby archway. There was a large chest and she ducked behind it.

"Take me to this prisoner then!" she heard King Rat snap.

Peeping out from behind the chest, Rosa saw a black rat with a golden crown on his head and a long purple cloak come marching across the hall. He looked really scary with his red eyes and curling whiskers. She hid back behind the chest as he headed for the steps that led to the room where she had been kept prisoner.

Oh no! As soon as he got there he would realise she had escaped!

She looked all around her. The chest was in a small corridor that seemed to be used for keeping bags of vegetables. Turning, she ran down it, her heart thudding. Any minute now, the guards would get out and come looking for her! What was she going to do?

Rosa's Plan

Rosa didn't know where she was going, but surely there must be a way out. She hurried down the corridor till she came to a small door in the wall. It looked like the door she had seen earlier from the outside of the castle. Her heart leaped. It was locked but there was a key in it!

She turned the lock and opened the door

and now she could see the woods just ahead of her! She ran towards them, faster than she had ever run in her life. With every stride she expected to hear voices shouting to stop and mice running after her but the only sound was of muffled yelling from inside the castle. She had a feeling her escape had just been discovered and the guards were in trouble but she didn't care. She had got out!

As she entered the woods, Nutmeg flew up to her. "Oh, Rosa! What happened?" The fairy looked scared stiff. "I saw the guards capture you. I didn't know what to do!"

"I'm really sorry," Rosa panted. "I was just trying to help the princess. I thought that if only I could get inside I might be able to hide and let her out tonight."

"It was really brave of you," Nutmeg said admiringly.

"It was really stupid," groaned Rosa. "I got locked in a room and I had to escape." She glanced around. "I think the guards might be after me at any moment."

"Quick, let's get out of here!" said Nutmeg. She grabbed Rosa's hand, waved her wand and spun in a pirouette. Silver and pink sparkles swirled around them and Rosa felt herself spinning round as Nutmeg's magic whisked them away.

They landed in a quiet clearing in the middle of the woods a safe distance away from the castle.

Rosa breathed out. "Phew!" She still had the key in her hand and her relief at escaping turned into excitement as she realised they now had a way to get into – and out of – the castle. She showed it to Nutmeg. "This opens the small door in the wall. We can use it to help Princess Cressida escape!" The fairy looked puzzled but a plan was already forming in Rosa's mind. "As soon as the princess comes back to her room, you can run up to the tower and sneak through the door. Then you and the princess can run downstairs and escape back out through the little door. If the guards come I'll distract them!"

"How?" asked Nutmeg.

"I don't know," Rosa admitted.

"Hmmm." Nutmeg started dancing to the

side, her feet crossing over quickly. Rosa recognised that it was a dance from *Swan Lake*. The fairy moved one way and then the other. "I always think better when I dance!" She spun round and then suddenly stopped, her eyes wide. "I know! I could use my magic to make you look exactly like the princess and teach you a dance she does! If the guards saw you

159

dancing at the edge of the woods it would trick them and they'd run after you – leaving the coast clear." She frowned. "But it would be really dangerous for you."

"I don't mind!" Rosa said bravely.

"It might work. If you could just distract them for a few minutes, Cressida and I could run to the woods and then I could magic us all away," said Nutmeg.

"Let's do it!" said Rosa. She looked at the sky. The sun was just starting to set. They had to be quick. "Can you teach me the dance now?"

Nutmeg waved her wand and beautiful music from *Swan Lake* filled the clearing. "Copy me!" Nutmeg danced three steps forwards before turning three times, one arm

above her head, one out to the side. Then she danced on in a big circle, turning with every step until she stopped in an arabesque, one leg held out behind her.

Rosa copied her. It felt wonderful to be dancing outside in the open air. She spun around letting the music flow through her. She didn't care if she got things a bit wrong; she just lost herself in the wonderful feeling. As she finished, she balanced on one leg.

Nutmeg looked very impressed. "You're really good at dancing, Rosa!"

Rosa smiled at her. "Thank you!" She felt even braver after the fairy's praise. "Do you think the mouse guards will have given up looking for me by now?"

"I should think so." Nutmeg nodded.

"Then let's go back to the castle!"

Nutmeg's magic took them to the edge of the forest… just as the sun was setting. The swan princess flapped her her wings and took off from the water.

Rosa watched the bird swoop into the tower.
A few minutes later, a girl in a white dress
appeared at the window. She had long
golden hair and looked sad.

"That's Cressida," said Nutmeg. "I'd better
make you look like her right away!"

Nutmeg began to dance around Rosa. A tingling started in Rosa's toes. It spread up her body and down her arms and up through her head. Nutmeg stopped and pointed her wand at her. There was a silver flash. Rosa blinked and gasped. Suddenly she was wearing a white dress. She put her hands to her head. She had a tiara on and her hair was now a deeper gold colour. "Oh, wow," she gasped. Nutmeg took a small mirror out of the pocket of her tutu and held it up. Rosa stared. Her own face wasn't looking back at her, but the face of the princess. It was a very weird feeling!

"How long will the magic last?" she asked quickly.

"Not long," said Nutmeg. "Some fairies in Enchantia can do transformation magic that lasts for hours but I'm still not very good at it. But it should last until Cressida and I escape." She rose into the air. "Good luck!"

"You too," called Rosa.

Nutmeg ran as fast as she could to the little door, and with one quick look back at Rosa, she disappeared inside.

Rosa took a deep breath. This was it! Nutmeg would hopefully be letting Princess Cressida out. *Oh, hurry up, hurry up*, she willed them. *Please get out before the guards come!*

"Hup two, hup two!"

It was too late. The guards were marching around the building. If Nutmeg and the princess opened the door now they'd be seen for sure!

Rosa didn't hesitate. Nutmeg and the princess were in danger. She had to help! Lifting her arms, she danced out of the trees…

Escape!

The two guards at the front of the group stopped so that the guards behind bumped into them. There was a chorus of "oofs" and "ouches" as tails were trodden on and swords tripped over.

"It's the princess!" the guards in the front shouted as Rosa danced.

Rosa's heart somersaulted as the guards

started charging towards her. She turned and ran into the dark trees.

"STOP!" the guards yelled.

No way, thought Rosa as she ran in and out of the trees, jumping over tree roots and stumps. The ballet shoes seemed to help her, making her feet move more lightly than ever as she twisted and turned on the forest paths. She glanced behind her. The guards were getting closer!

But Cressida and Nutmeg were also running across the grass towards the trees, aiming for a spot far to the right. Luckily the guards were so busy chasing Rosa that they didn't look behind them. They raced after her.

Rosa headed in the direction that Nutmeg

and Cressida were going but as she did so, she realised there was a wall of trees and bushes in front of her. There was no way through. She was trapped!

"We've got her!" screeched Mangy Tail.

Rosa turned around as the guards skidded to a halt behind her. They formed a semi-circle, swords pointing at her. She backed up until she was pressed against the trees.

"Come on, Princess," snarled Whiskers through the dusk. "I don't know how you escaped but you're coming back to the castle with us right now before King Rat finds out…" He blinked. Rosa felt herself tingling all over and glanced down. The magic was wearing off!

"What… what's happening?" The guards began to back off in alarm as Rosa felt herself change.

Suddenly someone grabbed her hand from behind the tree.

"We're here!" Nutmeg's voice whispered. Rosa's heart leaped.

"It's that girl!" said Mangy Tail suddenly.

Whiskers recovered from his confusion. "It's a trick again! GET HER!" He and the other guards leaped toward Rosa but at that very moment, Rosa felt Nutmeg's fingers tighten on hers.

"Hold on!" the fairy cried as a tinkling of music rang out.

And just as the guards' paws reached out to grab Rosa, a swirling curtain of silver and pink sparkles surrounded her and she felt herself being whisked away into the air, twirling round as if she was on a tea cup ride...

She landed a few seconds later. As the sparkles cleared, she realised that she was standing in a bedroom on a cream rug. Nutmeg was holding her right hand and Princess Cressida was holding her left.

"We... we escaped!" Rosa gasped.

"Only just," said Nutmeg, looking pale. "Oh, Rosa, that was so close!"

"Thank you so much for rescuing me!" Princess Cressida said, giving Rosa a hug as the bedroom door opened and a beautiful lady in a blue dress with a golden crown on her head looked in. "Oh my goodness!" she cried, stopping in her tracks. "Cressida! It's you!"

"Queen Isabella," said Nutmeg sinking into a deep curtsey. Rosa quickly followed her example.

Cressida however ran towards the Queen and hugged her. "I'm safe, Auntie! Rosa and Nutmeg rescued me! Oh, wait until you hear what happened!"

The Queen fetched the King and ten minutes later, Cressida and Nutmeg had told them everything. Rosa stood shyly at one side, not wanting to intrude. "Nutmeg used her magic to whisk us all back here," said Cressida, "and now we're safe!"

The Queen turned to Nutmeg and Rosa, grateful tears in her eyes. "Thank you, Nutmeg. And thank you, Rosa. You have both acted so bravely."

"I'm really glad I helped, but I did some

stupid things," admitted Rosa. "I should never have gone off into the castle on my own the first time. It could have turned out really, really badly." She sighed. "My mum's always saying I should think more before I do and say things."

And she's right, Rosa thought, reminding herself of Olivia.

The Queen smiled though. "Do not be too hard on yourself. It is good to act and not just think, good to be prepared to take risks, good to be brave for the sake of others. I think you are a worthy owner of the ballet shoes, Rosa." She took her hands. "I am very, very glad you have been chosen to wear them."

"I am too," said Rosa happily. The adventure might have been scary but it had also been really good fun!

"You must not tell anyone about your time here," warned the Queen. "Keep the red shoes' magic secret."

"We should have a feast and dancing to celebrate Rosa's first visit to Enchantia," King Tristan declared. "Let the party begin!"

The rest of the evening passed in a whirl of eating delicious food, dancing to lively tunes and having fun. As they stopped after an energetic polka at midnight, Rosa felt her feet

tingling. At first she thought it was just because she had been dancing so much but then she realised that her shoes were glowing again. "I think I'm about to go home!" she gasped.

"Come back soon!" called Nutmeg. "Bye, Rosa!"

"Goodbye!" called Princess Cressida.

The last thing Rosa saw was Nutmeg and Cressida smiling and waving and then colours swirled around her and she was swept away…

Friends Again

Rosa looked around. She was back in the changing rooms!

She took a deep trembling breath. She could hardly believe everything that had just happened. No wonder Madame Za-Za and Delphie had told her the ballet shoes were special!

Glancing at the clock on the wall, she

saw that it was exactly the same time as when she had gone away. It was weird to think that no time had passed here while she had been doing so much. *And now she had something else to do,* she reminded herself. *I'm going to go home and ring Olivia and say sorry.*

Just as she finished getting dressed, she heard the main door of the ballet school open. There was the sound of running feet and then the changing-rooms door opened too. Olivia ran in. She stopped when she saw Rosa. "I forgot my cardigan," she said briefly. Grabbing it from the bench, she went to leave.

"Wait!" Rosa burst out. "Olivia, I'm sorry!" The words tumbled out of her. "I shouldn't have got cross earlier. I was just angry because I'd wanted to show you round. But it was stupid of me to lose my temper – I'm just too impetuous – and I really didn't mean to bump into you in class. It was just an accident. I am really, really sorry. Can we be friends again?" She held her breath.

But she needn't have worried. Olivia smiled almost instantly. "Of course we can."

Rosa felt a rush of relief.

"Do you want to come to mine for tea?" said Olivia. "We could stop at your house on the way and ask your mum if it's OK."

"Yes, please!" Even though Rosa knew she couldn't tell Olivia about Enchantia, she suddenly realised she could share her adventures with her in a different way. "There's this new dance I've learned. It's from *Swan Lake*. I could teach you it."

"That sounds cool," said Olivia. "Let's go!"

Rosa picked up her things. As she looked at the red ballet shoes she stopped and smiled to herself. *Thank you for the shoes, Delphie,* she thought.

She'd had an amazing time in Enchantia. When would she go again? And what would happen next time? Feeling excited, she put the shoes in her bag and ran after Olivia.

Tiptoe over the page to learn

a special dance step...

Darcey's Magical Masterclass

The Swan Lake Glide

The swans are some of the most elegant creatures in Enchantia. Try this running movement and see if you can be as elegant as they are and imagine your arms are like wings...

1.
Stand on your tiptoes with your arms held out to the side.

2.
Take little steps forwards whilst still on tiptoes, starting slowly and then move into a gentle, graceful run.

3.
Make your arms soft in the elbow and flap them gently up and down as if preparing for flight.

4.
Finish with a small jump into the air.

Magic
Ballerina™
Rosa and the Golden Bird

The Wicked Fairy has captured the magical
Firebird and stopped any music playing in
Enchantia! Can Rosa help her friends to
dance once more?

**Read on for a sneak preview
of Rosa and the Golden Bird...**

Rosa heard the sound of voices carrying through the still air. They were raised and angry. Through the trees, there was a small group of people. One of them was a slim fairy in a pale pink and brown tutu. Nutmeg!

Rosa's heart leaped at the sight of her friend. She began to run but as she got closer, she saw that the group were arguing with a large fairy wearing a black dress and a long cloak. Her grey hair was in a bun and she had a hooked nose and warts. She looked very scary. Rosa stopped at the edge of the clearing.

"Please let the Firebird go," one of the men in the group was pleading with her.

"No!" snapped the fairy.

"But you can't just keep him in a cage. It's mean and the birds in the forest need to be able to sing again!" said Nutmeg. "You have to release him!"

The fairy glared at her. "Have to! No one tells me I have to do anything. I will do exactly as I please!"

"No you won't!" cried Nutmeg. She stepped forward towards the fairy, hands on her hips. "We'll stop you!"

"Oh you will, will you? Well, we'll soon see about that!" There was a flash of light and a loud crack.

Rosa's hands flew to her mouth. The four people in front of the fairy were suddenly as still as statues. She had turned them all to stone!

°⊙·*·☆·⊙·*·☆·⊙·*·☆·⊙·*·°

Darcey Bussell

Buy more great Magic Ballerina books direct from
HarperCollins at 10% off recommended retail price.
FREE postage and packing in the UK.

All priced at £3.99

Buy more great Magic Ballerina books direct from
HarperCollins at 10% off recommended retail price.
FREE postage and packing in the UK.

Rosa and the Secret Princess	ISBN 978 0 00 730029 7
Rosa and the Golden Bird	ISBN 978 0 00 730030 3
Rosa and the Magic Moonstone	ISBN 978 0 00 730031 0
Rosa and the Special Prize	ISBN 978 0 00 730032 7
Rosa and the Magic Dream	ISBN 978 0 00 730033 4
Rosa and the Three Wishes	ISBN 978 0 00 730034 1
Holly and the Dancing Cat	ISBN 978 0 00 732319 7
Holly and the Silver Unicorn	ISBN 978 0 00 732320 3
Holly and the Magic Tiara	ISBN 978 0 00 732321 0
Holly and the Rose Garden	ISBN 978 0 00 732322 7
Holly and the Ice Palace	ISBN 978 0 00 732323 4
Holly and the Land of Sweets	ISBN 978 0 00 732324 1

All priced at £3.99

To purchase by Visa/Mastercard/Maestro simply call
08707871724 or fax on **08707871725**

Darcey Bussell

Buy more great Magic Ballerina books direct from
HarperCollins at 10% off recommended retail price.
FREE postage and packing in the UK.

Jade and the Enchanted Wood	ISBN 978 0 00 734875 6
Jade and the Surprise Party	ISBN 978 0 00 734876 3
Jade and the Silver Flute	ISBN 978 0 00 734877 0
Jade and the Carnival	ISBN 978 0 00 734878 7

All priced at £3.99

To purchase by Visa/Mastercard/Maestro simply call
08707871724 or fax on **08707871725**

To pay by cheque, send a copy of this form with a cheque made payable to
'HarperCollins Publishers' to: Mail Order Dept. (Ref: BOB4),
HarperCollins Publishers, Westerhill Road, Bishopbriggs, G64 2QT,
making sure to include your full name, postal address and phone number.

From time to time HarperCollins may wish to use your personal data
to send you details of other HarperCollins publications and offers.
If you wish to receive information on other HarperCollins publications
and offers please tick this box ☐

Do not send cash or currency. Prices correct at time of press.
Prices and availability are subject to change without notice.
Delivery overseas and to Ireland incurs a £2 per book postage and packing charge.